KU-067-978

Wolf Hill

The Exploding Parrot

Roderick Hunt

Illustrated by Alex Brychta

Oxford University Press

Oxford University Press, Great Clarendon Street, Oxford, OX2 6DP

Oxford   New York
Athens   Auckland   Bangkok   Bogota   Buenos Aires   Calcutta
Cape Town   Chennai   Dar es Salaam   Delhi   Florence   Hong Kong
Istanbul   Karachi   Kuala Lumpur   Madrid   Melbourne   Mexico City
Mumbai   Nairobi   Paris   São Paulo   Singapore   Taipei   Tokyo
Toronto   Warsaw

and associated companies in
Berlin   Ibadan

Oxford is a trade mark of Oxford University Press

© text Roderick Hunt 1998
© illustrations Alex Brychta
First Published 1998

ISBN 019918667 7

Printed in Hong Kong

Chapter 1

Mr Gray got out of his digger. He scratched his head.

'Hey, Pete,' he called. 'Come and look at this.'

The other man came across.

'I've just dug it up,' said Mr Gray.
'What do you think it is?'

It lay on a pile of dirt and old
bricks. It was big and heavy. It looked
like a big tube. It had a pointed end.
It was made of metal but it was rusty
and caked with mud. Pete touched it
with his foot. It rocked gently from
side to side.

Mr Gray pushed away some dirt
and broken bricks.

'Look,' he said. 'There are fins on
this end.'

The object slid off the bricks and rolled over. Then it began to tick like a clock.

Mr Gray's face went white. 'Run for it! Quick!' he said. 'It's a bomb!'

Chapter 2

The phone rang. Mr Saffrey picked it up.

'Hello,' he said. 'This is Wolf Hill School.'

A voice spoke. Mr Saffrey listened. 'A bomb? Close to the school?' he said. 'Is this a joke?'

The voice spoke again. Mr Saffrey gulped. His face went pale.

'I see. It's an emergency,' he said.

'I have to get everybody out. And the bomb could go off at any second?'

Mr Saffrey put the phone down. He pressed the alarm bell. Then he ran out of his office.

Chapter 3

Miss Teal's class was in the hall.

Kat sighed. Her team was losing. Gizmo was in her team. Gizmo tried, but he just couldn't catch a ball.

'Throw!' shouted Miss Teal. Kat threw the ball. Najma caught it. Everyone ran.

'Stop!' shouted Miss Teal. Everyone stopped.

'Throw!' she shouted.

Najma threw the ball to Gizmo. It was a long, hard throw. It flew towards Gizmo. 'This is my chance to get it,' he thought.

The alarm bell began to ring.

Gizmo shut his eyes and dived. The ball smacked into his hand. It was an amazing catch. It was the best catch of his life.

Nobody saw Gizmo's amazing catch.

Mr Saffrey ran into the hall just as Gizmo caught the ball.

'Bomb alert!' he shouted. 'Get outside, now!'

Chapter 4

Everything happened at once. Everyone had to get out of the school quickly. Miss Teal's class were still in their PE clothes. There wasn't time to change.

They had to go to the sports centre.

The sports centre was a mile from the school. It was a long walk. Two police cars raced past them. Next came a fire engine, then two ambulances.

The children went in twos. Some of them held hands. None of them spoke. They were all too frightened.

There were red and white cones at the end of Mill Street.

A policewoman was stopping cars. 'It's a bomb alert,' she was saying. 'The area is being sealed off.'

Kat felt cold. She held Gizmo's hand.

'Did you see my catch?' whispered Gizmo.

'What did you say?' asked Kat.

'Nothing,' said Gizmo. 'It doesn't matter.'

Chapter 5

At the sports centre, Mr Saffrey made everyone sit on the floor. Then the teachers checked that nobody was missing. It took ages.

'I'm freezing. I wish we knew what was going on,' said Chris.

A policewoman came into the hall.
She spoke to Mr Saffrey. Mr Saffrey
nodded. Then he clapped his hands.
'Quiet, everybody,' he said. 'This is
Inspector Webb. She will tell you
what is happening.'

Inspector Webb smiled, but her face
looked serious.

'A bomb has been found near the school,' she said. 'It's a World War Two bomb. It could explode. We have to make it safe. I'm afraid it may take a long time.'

'Nobody knows how long,' said Mr Saffrey. 'I'm sorry. Some of you can't go home until it's safe.'

Chapter 6

The police went to every house.
They knocked on every door.

'Lock up,' they said, 'and go to the
sports centre.'

'I can't. I'm cooking liver,' said
Loz's Gran. 'I'll come later.'

'No, you won't,' said the policeman.
'This is serious. You must come now.'

The police took Gran to the sports centre. Other people began to arrive too. Najma's mum came with Adel and the baby. So did Gizmo's dad. Kat's mum arrived with a towel on her head.

Some of the children didn't live close to the bomb. They went home with their parents. Chris went to his uncle's house in Walton Street.

Later, a lorry arrived. Soldiers began to bring beds into the hall.

'Oh no!' said Kat 'You know what that means. We're going to be here all night!'

Arjo grinned. He liked the idea.

Chapter 7

The grown-ups were upset.

'All night!' said Gizmo's dad. 'Who wants to sleep here all night?'

'We won't get much sleep,' said
Kat's mum.

'No, I'd rather go home,' said Loz's
Gran.

'It's like the War, all over again,' said
Mr Morgan. 'I can remember the
bombs falling.'

Mr Morgan's dog began to scratch. 'I must get him some flea shampoo,' he said.

Mrs Martin grabbed Jamie-Lee's hand. 'Fleas! I'm not sleeping here,' she said. 'Come on, Terry. We're going to a hotel.'

Mr Martin sighed.

Everyone started to make their beds.

'May I sleep next to Najma?' asked Kat.

'I suppose so,' said Najma's mum.

Suddenly Kat's mum gasped. 'Oh no!' she said. 'I've just remembered something.'

'What?' asked Kat.

'Auntie Viv's parrot,' said Kat's mum. 'I left it behind!'

Chapter 8

Everything was quiet in Wolf Street. Two soldiers walked up the street. They looked at the numbers on the doors.

'This is it,' said one of the soldiers.
'Number 12.'

The other soldier laughed. He put
on a funny voice. 'Our job is to
rescue Auntie Viv's parrot,' he said.
'This is an important mission. We
must not fail!'

The first soldier sniffed. 'Can you smell something?' he asked.

'I'm not sure,' said the other soldier.

'Come on,' said the first soldier. 'Let's get the parrot and get out.'

The other soldier had a key. He unlocked the door.

A terrible smell hit them. It was gas.

Chapter 9

'Quick!' said the first soldier. 'It's the gas cooker! You turn it off. Then open the windows. I'll find the parrot.'

The first soldier looked around. The parrot wasn't in its cage.

The other soldier turned the gas
off. Then he opened the windows.
They still couldn't find the parrot.

'That's funny,' said the first soldier.
'The cage door is open. But where's
the parrot?'

'It may be dead,' said the other soldier. 'Perhaps the gas killed it.'

The parrot wasn't dead. It was hiding behind the sofa.

Suddenly it squawked. Then it flew up, flapping its wings.

'Grab it!' shouted the first soldier.

The parrot flew towards the window. 'Come back!' shouted the other soldier.

It was too late. Auntie Viv's parrot flew out of the open window. It flew over the rooftops. Up, up it flew. The soldiers watched it. At last it was out of sight.

Chapter 10

Mr Saffrey said, 'I'm afraid there's good news and bad news.'

'Tell us the bad news first,' said Kat's mum.

Mr Saffrey told them that the parrot had flown away.

Kat was upset. 'It's not our parrot,' she said. 'It belongs to my Auntie Viv. We're looking after it.'

'What happened?' asked Kat's mum. Mr Saffrey told them about the gas.

'You must have left it on. The soldiers had to open the windows. The parrot flew away.'

'What will happen to it?' asked Kat.

'Maybe someone will catch it,' said Mr Saffrey, 'or maybe it will fly back.'

'I hope so,' said Kat. 'Auntie Viv loves that parrot. How are we going to tell her?'

'What's the good news?' asked Kat's Mum.

'Well,' said Mr Saffrey. 'You left the gas on. At least your house didn't blow up.'

Chapter 11

'Phew!' said Captain Jones. 'So far, so good.'

Captain Jones hated bombs. 'I can't think why I do this job,' he said.

'You like the danger,' said Corporal Smith.

Captain Jones looked at the bomb.
'This is the tricky bit,' he said. 'Pass
me those clippers.'

Corporal Smith held his breath.
Then he crossed his fingers.
Suddenly there was a flapping sound.
It was a parrot. It flew down and
landed on the bomb.

Captain Jones gasped.

'A nice cup of tea!' said the parrot.

Corporal Smith waved his hands. 'Shoo! Shoo! Go away,' he said.

The parrot didn't want to fly away.
It put its head on one side.

'Give us a kiss,' it said.

Chapter 12

It was late at night. People were sitting on the beds. Only the very small children were asleep. Kat and Najma were still talking.

Kat's mum said, 'It's midnight. I think you two should go to bed. You'll be tired.'

'We'll never sleep,' said Kat.

Suddenly the doors of the hall opened. Inspector Webb came in with Captain Jones and Corporal Smith. The soldiers were covered in mud.

'Good news, everyone,' said Inspector Webb. She grinned at the soldiers. 'The bomb is safe. Thanks to these two, you can all go home.'

Everyone cheered and clapped.

Corporal Jones was holding a box. 'We had to take a prisoner,' he said.

A voice came from the box. 'Give us a kiss,' it said.

Chapter 13

There were pictures in all the newspapers. They showed Auntie Viv's parrot sitting on the bomb. Another showed it on Corporal Smith's shoulder.

One said,

Bomb disposal team get the bird.

Another said,

Parrot in bomb drama

The newspapers told how the parrot landed on the bomb.

'It was a tricky moment,' said Captain Jones. 'Defusing a bomb with a tame parrot on it is not easy. It was a good job the bomb didn't explode. It would have made a real mess of the parrot!'

Auntie Viv's parrot was famous. Reporters came to Kat's house in Wolf Street. They all wanted to talk to Kat's mum. One of them even wanted to interview the parrot.

'I don't know what Auntie Viv is going say,' said Kat.

Chapter 14

Kat was with Loz, Andy and Gizmo. They were working in the computer room. They were writing a story for the class newspaper.

'What can we write about?' asked Loz.

'How about the bomb?' said Andy.

'We've done that before,' said Kat.

'Write about your Auntie Viv's parrot,' said Gizmo.

'But I want something different,' said Kat.

'Write the story as if you were the parrot,' he suggested.

'Brilliant!' said Kat. 'That's what we'll do.'

She began with, 'My Adventure, by Nelson the Parrot. I am a parrot who loves exploring . . .'

Loz laughed. 'You've made a mistake, Kat. Look!'

Kat had typed, 'I am a parrot who loves exploding.'

'The exploding parrot!' said Andy. 'I like that. It's a great title for the story!'